Adapted by Scott Ciencin

Based on the series created by

Mark McCorkle & Bob Schooley

New York

Printed in the United States of America

First Edition
1 3 5 7 9 10 8 6 4 2

Library of Congress Catalog Card Number on file.

ISBN 0-7868-4629-1

CHAPTER 1

Desert Desperados

A mysterious car drove along the desert's broiling hot sand. When it reached a large cactus, the vehicle stopped. A window rolled down. A gloved hand stretched out, and a stolen security card flashed.

Bing! announced the fake cactus after reading the card. In the sand ahead, a trap-door opened. The car drove into the dark tunnel and down a long ramp.

Company had arrived. *Bad* company.

* * *

Inside the secret underground lab, a bored guard sat at the front desk. He didn't notice anyone *bad* coming in. He was too busy watching a baseball game on TV.

"Hey, Frank," said the guard when he heard footsteps, "ya got my iced mocha?"

"Maybe ya oughta lay off the caffeine," said the evil Shego, looming over him. "It keeps you awake."

The raven-haired villain tapped her clawed finger on the guard's forehead. After a bright emerald flash, the guard slumped to his desk.

Shego's evil-genius boss, Dr. Drakken, boldly strolled through the doorway. "Well done, Shego," he said.

"Dr. Drakken! Stop!" cried Shego.

"*I* give the orders. *You* do not tell me to stop," he snapped and smugly kept walking.

"I do when I haven't shut down the alarm system yet," said Shego.

An ear-piercing alarm bell blared. The mad scientist nearly leaped out of his blue skin!

Steel doors slid open, and a squad of security troops rushed forward.

Shego stretched out her arms. Her energy claws glowed fiercely. With a savage cry, she surged at the troopers.

Bam! Slam! Wham!

Shego unleashed a flurry of high jump

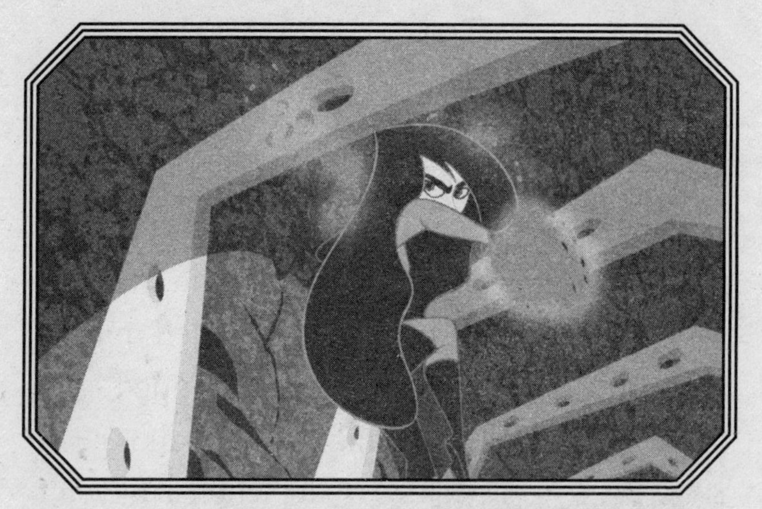

kicks, knee and elbow strikes, and scissor spear-finger thrusts.

One trooper after another dropped. In mere seconds, Shego stood atop a heap of defeated foes.

Drakken checked his watch. “Can we pick up the pace?” he asked.

Shego glared at her boss, flipped in midair, and landed in front of him.

“You’re the one who set off the alarm!” she snarled. “Let’s just steal your stupid whatever-it-is and get out of here.”

"That back talk is what slows down our entire operation," said Drakken. "I demand obedience!"

Shego laughed. "From me? *Please!*"

Drakken watched her strut away. But he didn't get angry. Oh, no. "If my latest scheme works," he muttered to himself, "*obedience* is what I shall have."

Then he unleashed the evilest of evil-genius laughs. "*Ha-ha-ha-ha-ha-ha-ha-ha! Ha-ha-ha-ha-ha-ha-ha-ha! Ha-ha-ha-ha-ha-ha-ha-ha . . .*"

(And he went on like that for a *really* long time.)

Punked!

In the upstairs bathroom of the Possible home, crime-fighter Kim had turned *grime* fighter.

First, she applied an icky cream mask to her face. Then, with toothbrush in hand, she waged a ferocious war on tooth decay.

"Kim!" cried a voice from behind.

As Kim whirled, Tim Possible blasted her with his air horn!

HONK! HONK! HONK!

Kim grimaced—and couldn't have looked freakier if she tried. Her eyes bugged out. And white cream covered her face.

BOOSH! A blinding flash seared her vision. When her eyes cleared, she saw the digital camera in her little brother's hand.

"Gimme that!" Kim demanded.

"Sure," said Tim. After popping out a tiny disk, he tossed the camera in the air.

Scrambling, Kim caught the camera and ran after her brother.

Tim raced into the bedroom he shared with his identical twin. He tossed the disk to Jim, who stood beside their computer.

"What are you *doing*?" Kim cried.

But it was too late to stop them. Jim slammed the disk home and pressed the

SEND key. In a flash, the computer screen displayed a picture of Kim looking bug-eyed and moon-faced.

Kim rolled her eyes. "So what?" she said. "I'm your new screen saver?"

"You're *everybody's* new screen saver," declared Jim.

"We wrote an e-mail program that beamed it to *everyone* in Middleton," boasted Tim.

"Oh, right," Kim said. "Like you jokers have the brains to write a program like—"

Kim's cell phone rang. She whipped it from her big jammie pocket. "Hello?"

"Hi, Kim, it's *Bonnie*," came the familiar *un*friendly voice of her fellow cheerleader Bonnie Rockwaller.

"Uh, hi . . ." said Kim.

"Is that zit cream? Or should I, like, call a paramedic?" said Bonnie, barely holding back her laughter.

Tweebs! thought Kim. They *had* broadcast that gross picture. Her two little punk brothers had punked her!

"It's moisturizer, Bonnie," snapped Kim. Then she stabbed the phone's OFF button and glared at her tweeby brothers.

The two threw her their best "sweet and innocent" smiles.

Yuh-huh, right, thought Kim. "Don't think you're off the hook," she warned.

Just then, her Kimmunicator trilled.

"Hey, Wade," she said, answering. "What's the sitch?"

Wade was the ten-year-old computer genius who ran Kim's I CAN DO ANYTHING Web site.

"Drakken and Shego just raided a top secret research facility in the Southwest," Wade said from the Kimmunicator's tiny view screen.

"Can you set up a ride for tomorrow?" Kim asked.

"Already set," Wade assured her. "The lab is sending their plane."

Kim's mood brightened. A mission meant two days *without* the terrible twosome.

"Cool! Anything else?" she asked.

Wade swung one of his computer screens around. Kim's goofy, cream-faced picture was *plastered* across it.

"Yeah," he said. "Next time, rinse your face before they take the picture!"

"Urgh!" Fuming, Kim snapped off the Kimmunicator and stormed out.

The twins' wicked laughter followed her all the way back to her room.

CHAPTER 3

Excess Baggage

The next morning, Kim dragged herself into the kitchen. With a yawn, she slumped into a chair at the breakfast table—and frowned.

On her plate were two fried eggs set like buggy eyes. Below them was a goofy bacon-strip smile.

She was *so* not in the mood for her mother's smiley face food art.

Kim's mom burst into the kitchen. Kim's

dad was right behind her. Both were dressed for the great outdoors.

"Morning, Kimmie," Kim's Mom called. "I made you a big breakfast."

Kim's Dad nodded. "Gotta carb up for the adventure that lies ahead."

Kim lazily lifted the bacon-strip "smile" off her breakfast face. "Just a break-in at a top secret lab," she said. "*So* not the drama."

"Break-in?" asked her dad.

"Top secret lab?" added her mom.

"We were talking about babysitting the twins," said Kim's father.

"Babysitting?" Kim's eyes widened. The

bacon strip slipped from her hand and landed—in a frown.

"We've got our spousal encounter today. Remember?" said Kim's mom.

Kim felt alarm bells ringing inside her head. "Oh, the thing at Lake Middleton?" she asked. "That's *today*?"

"You betcha," declared Kim's dad as he snatched a tackle box from the kitchen counter. "Your mother and I get to reconnect emotionally and do some serious fly-fishing."

Kim's mom smiled sweetly. "I'm not sure who picked the venue, but it should be fun."

Dr. Possible plopped a fly-fishing hat on his wife, and said, "Hon, don't forget your hat."

Kim looked away. "Um, speaking of forgetting," she said, "I totally spaced on the babysitting."

"Kimmie, you made a commitment," said her mother in a firm voice.

"*Two* commitments, actually," said Kim. "I'm supposed to go on a mission today."

Kim's father hitched up a pair of knee-high fishing boots. "You'll just have to take the boys."

Kim shuddered and wailed, "Mom, can you *please* tell Dad that's a bad idea."

But Kim's mother shook her head. "Oh, Kimmie," she said. "I'm sure Jim and Tim would *love* to visit a top secret lab with you."

Kim's shoulders sagged. *"Fine,"* she said. Then she rose from the table and dragged herself upstairs. "Like I can really take those two with me on a mission," she muttered. "Ugh, they're such—"

Reaching the landing, Kim shrieked.

Her room had been ransacked!

"Little freaks!" she hissed. "I am about to become an only child." She charged back downstairs. "Jim! Tim!"

She skidded to a stop near the front door. Her folks were standing there, about to leave.

Kim forced a smile. "Bye, Mom. Bye, Dad," she called.

"See you tonight, Kimmie," Kim's mother

said cheerfully. "And thanks for watching the boys."

Her dad grinned and added, "Have fun on your mission now, but easy on the snacks! Remember, candy is dandy, but fruit helps you poop!"

With a fading smile, Kim waved. "Fruit. Check," she said.

The second the door shut, her smile became a grimace. She rushed to Jim and Tim's room and cried, "You trashed my room!"

Tim blinked and held up the remains of her Kimmunicator. "We needed your tri-lithium power cell," he said. "Here, you can have the rest back."

"You destroyed my Kimmunicator?" Kim wailed. "To make some stupid *toy*?"

Jim presented the small device, which looked like a garage door opener. "It's not a toy," he protested. "It's a silicon phase disruptor."

"Handheld," Tim noted.

Kim grabbed it and shook it. "Give me back my batteries, you tweebs!" she cried.

"I'm not a dweeb," said Jim.

"Tweeb," Kim corrected. "Twin dweeb. Dweeb times two!"

With a sigh, Kim took back the batteries and stormed out of the twins' room.

This, she thought, is going to be the longest Saturday in Possible history!

A half hour later, Kim's best friend, Ron Stoppable, was sitting in her room.

Ron had tried to fix her busted Kimmunicator. But he was stumped—

"We may never be able to talk to Wade again," he moaned.

"Gimme!" said Rufus, Ron's pet naked mole rat. And he started working on it.

Kim sighed. "Ron, why can't my brothers be normal?"

"They're *relatively* normal," Ron assured her. "For twins, I mean. At least they don't speak their own weirdo language."

At that very moment, in the next room, Jim and Tim were talking.

"Hick-a-bick-a-boo?" asked Jim.

"Hoooo-shaaa," answered Tim.

Back in Kim's room, Kim was now pacing. "They're just so . . ." She shuddered. *Ugh!* "Like a ten-year-old could build a phase disruptor . . . or whatever it is."

"*Wade's* ten years old," Ron noted, "and he builds all sorts of stuff."

"Wade's a super-genius," said Kim. "He aced high school and college in, like, eight months."

"Maybe they're just pacing themselves. Like *me*," suggested Ron.

Just then, Rufus held out the Kimmunicator to Kim with a grand flourish and cried, "Ta-da!"

He'd fixed it! "Thank you, Rufus," said Kim.

Outside, a horn honked. "Oh, that must be our ride," she said.

A few minutes later, a sleek, experimental aircraft pointed its thrusters down and landed on the street.

Have Tweebs, Will Travel

The plane flew high in the sky above the Southwest desert. Inside the cockpit, Kim sat beside the big, friendly pilot with a neck like a tree trunk.

"Thanks for letting me bring along the terrible two, Mr. Geminini," Kim said.

The pilot shrugged. "How bad could they be?" he asked.

Hoping the man would never find out, Kim lost herself in the fluffy clouds ahead.

* * *

Back in the plane's cargo area, Ron was belted into a folding jump seat next to Kim's twin brothers.

Jim Possible pointed at one of the hoses lining the fuselage. "Where does this hose go?" he asked.

Ron shrugged. "To the back of the plane."

"What does it do?" Tim wanted to know.

Ron had just the answer for him: "Airplane stuff."

"Is it pneumatic or hydraulic?" Jim asked with a frustrated scowl.

"It's *I-don't-knowic,*" snapped Ron. *And I don't care-ic*, he added to himself.

Jim whispered to his brother, "Check it out."

"Got to," Tim said with a nod.

The curious twins twisted around in their seat belts.

"What are you guys doing?" asked Ron. He was suddenly ready to care—and very, *very* worried. . . .

Up in the cockpit, Kim pressed one of the Kimmunicator's buttons, hoping to contact Wade. *Sproing!* The broken button sprang back at her. Kim fumed.

"I have a twin brother," the pilot told her. "We were quite a handful, let me tell ya. But I turned out okay."

"What about your brother?" asked Kim.

Mr. Geminini chuckled. "Oh, he'll get out in five years with good behavior."

Suddenly, an alarm blared from the control panel. And the plane took a nosedive!

* * *

"Hey, don't touch that!" cried Ron back in the cargo area.

But it was too late. The twins had messed with the hose, and the plane had gone into a steep dive.

"Kim! They touched!" Ron yelled.

Mr. Geminini struggled with the stick. "We've got a major malfunction!" he shouted.

Two voices chirped up from the cargo area. "Sorry, Kim!"

Through gritted teeth, Kim noted, "*Two* major malfunctions."

And if Kim didn't act fast, they were going to crash!

"Tweebs!" Kim snarled as she stumbled back to the cargo area of the wildly spinning plane.

Next to Ron, the twins sunk low in their seats. Rufus dangled from an oxygen mask.

Panting, Kim reached them. "Jim! Tim!"

"We just wanted to know what was in that hose," said Jim.

"Why?" demanded Kim.

"Because it was there," said Tim.

Jim nodded at his brother, satisfied with his answer. "It was hydraulic fluid," he noted.

Kim couldn't *believe* these two. "And what better way to find out?" she snapped.

With a sigh, Kim kept moving toward the back of the plane. Finally, she saw the loose hose. It was whipping around in two pieces and spewing hydraulic fluid.

Kim lunged for it, but the hose slipped out of her grasp. She tried again and again, but nothing worked!

Finally, Kim fired her grappling hook at the side of the plane. Using it, she reeled herself to the hose, seized the ends, and sealed them together.

"Gotcha!" Kim yelled.

In the cockpit, a pale and shaky Mr. Geminini clutched the controls. The alarm went silent, and he was able to pull the plane out of its deadly dive.

Back in the cargo bay, Rufus let go of his oxygen mask and fell into Ron's hands. "*Phew!*" he cried.

CHAPTER 5

Boys Will Be Boys

Soon the plane was safely on the ground, and Kim was walking into the desert lab's secret entrance.

"Kim *Possible* . . ." said the white-haired scientist, shaking her hand. "Thank you for coming! I'm Dr. Cyrus Bortle."

Jim and Tim raced forward.

"A secret lab!" Jim cried.

"Check it out!" exclaimed Tim.

Ron pulled Kim aside and said, "Those

two in a top secret lab? This could be a bigger threat to the free world than Drakken."

Kim glared at her brothers and declared, "Not *could be*. Definitely."

Dr. Bortle led them to his workshop at the heart of the lab. They all gathered around the gold-plated safe. Its shredded door looked like it had been clawed open.

Rufus chittered busily as he checked out the safe's door. Ron and Kim examined the claw marks, too.

"Shego?" they asked together.

"Ah-huh, Shego," agreed the mole rat.

"Dr. Bortle?" called Kim. When the doctor did not answer, she turned.

"Boys, please!" wailed the doctor. He was trying to shoo Jim and Tim off a big square machine.

Kim sighed. "Here we go."

Waving his finger, the scientist scolded, "That's a *very* delicate piece of equipment called a—"

"Silicon phase disruptor," Jim stated.

"How did you know that?" Dr. Bortle asked.

Tim whipped out their handheld model. "We're making one *too*."

"Except mine is *real*," said Dr. Bortle.

"So is ours!" claimed the twins.

"A handheld unit?" Dr. Bortle snickered. "It is simply not possible."

"Anything's *possible*—" declared Tim.

"—for a Possible," Jim finished.

Dr. Bortle mussed Tim's hair. "Boys, boys, boys. You know, when I was a boy I liked to make believe I was making rocket ships and blaster rays."

"But we *do* make rockets," said Jim.

"*And* blaster rays," added Tim.

Dr. Bortle sighed. He turned to Kim and shrugged. "Mmm. Such cute lads."

"Doctor, what *exactly* was in the safe?" Kim asked.

"My latest project: the neural compliance chip," he said.

Ron's brow furrowed in confusion. "Uh. . . . Let's *pretend* I don't know what that is," he said.

"It's a microcomputer that overrides the brain and the nervous system," Jim explained.

"Total mind control," added Tim.

But Kim didn't believe them. "Um, I don't think so," she told her brothers. "That would be like ferociously unethical. Dr. Bortle would *not* invent something like that. Right?"

"Well, *ferociously unethical* is a little

harsh," said Dr. Bortle with a sheepish chuckle.

"Drakken has total mind control power?!" squealed Ron. *Freak me out!* he thought.

On Ron's shoulder, Rufus whimpered, "Oh, man!"

Kim's eyes narrowed at the thought of Drakken's plans. "Yet another take-over-the-world thing," she guessed.

Ron nodded. "That *or* he's gonna force people to listen to those stories about his twisted childhood."

CHAPTER 6

Scene of the Slime

At that very moment, in a faraway lair, Dr. Drakken was committing an act of unspeakable horror. His victim was Shego.

"Then in fourth grade, I developed a ray that allowed me to control rubber products," Drakken rambled as he paced about his secret lab. "They said I was *mad.* But after that, no one could best me in four-square, tetherball, or even . . ."

Drakken spun and raised his clenched

fist. ". . . dodge ball. Isn't that fascinating?"

Shego held a tray of milk and cookies, a blank look on her face.

"Fascinating, Dr. Drakken," she said sweetly. On her forehead, a postage stamp-sized *compliance chip* glowed deep red.

"Want to hear more exciting stories from my formative years? Hmm?" Drakken asked.

"Yes, Dr. Drakken," Shego said in the same sickly sweet tone.

He waved his hand. "No time," he said. "I have to make more chips if I want the whole world to be blindly obedient to me. And you know I do, Shego."

"Yes, Dr. Drakken," she chanted.

Drakken smiled madly. Shego was only

his first victim. With this technology, he was going to rule the world . . . and *everyone* in it!

* * *

Back in Dr. Bortle's underground lab, Kim rummaged through her backpack.

"Miss Possible, Miss Possible, Miss Possible, *please*," protested Dr. Bortle. "Our security officers have searched the lab already."

Kim yanked a case from her bag. "*They* don't have spectrometer sunglasses," she noted.

She slipped on the sleek and oh-so-*stylin'* glasses. A tiny arm snaked free of the frames and gave off a purple beam.

"Fascinating," Dr. Bortle admitted. "Where'd you get those?"

"Ten-year-old super-genius," Kim replied.

"Your brothers?" asked the doctor.

Kim glared at him over the glasses. "So *not*," she said.

Pushing the glasses back in place, she scanned the lab. Wherever the beam tracked, glowing purple fingerprints and footprints were revealed.

Near the safe, Kim spotted a boot print that clearly belonged to Shego. But it had a weird orange glow near one edge—

"Got something?" asked Ron.

Kim took out a tiny set of tweezers and picked up a fragment of something weird.

"Maybe," Kim murmured. She needed help. "Hmm, Wade? Are you getting this?"

Everything she saw through the glasses was broadcast to one of Wade's computers.

"It's a leaf," said Wade, "or a piece of one." He tapped a few keys and glanced at his data. "Oh! From the Cuahotoc fern."

"And I'm betting they don't grow in the desert," said Kim.

"They don't grow *anywhere*," replied Wade, "except at the foot of Tashiyu Falls located in the Peruvian rain forest."

Kim took off the glasses.

"Okay," said Kim to Ron and Rufus, "so we go to Peru, find Drakken, grab the compliance chip, and get the tweebs back home before dinner."

Later that day, a silver jet soared high above a South American jungle. Two skydivers leaped from the plane—Kim and Ron.

The two were now experiencing the heady rush of free fall—with a *tweeb* strapped to each of them!

Ron looked down. The ground was rushing up at them. And he did not like heights. No he did *not*. "Isn't it time to pull our chutes?" he asked nervously.

"No way!" Tim's flailing hands kept Ron from opening the parachute. "Freefalling is *cool*!"

"Kim!" shouted the freaked-out Ron.

She rocketed through the air and pulled his rip cord for him. *Fwooop!* Ron's chute opened. And his mouth closed.

In minutes they were all on the ground, carving their way through the dense jungle. As the sound of rushing water grew louder, Kim guided them into a clearing.

The five-hundred-foot-high Tashiyu Falls appeared before them. Kim stared up at it.

Ron scratched his head, not sure what he was supposed to be looking for. "I see . . . water?" he mumbled.

Kim pulled out her Kimmunicator and aimed it at the falls. Wade's image appeared.

"Tech scan it, Wade," said Kim.

Wade's fingers flashed across his keyboard.

"Getting anything?" asked Kim.

"Huge energy readings," Wade informed her. "Halfway up."

"There's probably an entrance behind the falls," said Kim. "Thanks, Wade."

Ron frowned. "Why are the entrances never just, you know, like, a door?" he asked.

Kim readied her grappling hook. "Okay, Ron," she said. "*I'll* infiltrate Drakken's lair

and get the chip. *You* keep an eye on the tweebs."

Ron looked over his shoulder. Tim was imitating a crazed monkey, hanging upside down from a vine. Jim was about to join him.

He turned back to Kim. "Oh sure," he said, "give *me* the dangerous assignment."

"But we want to go, too!" Tim cried. He flipped over and dropped to the ground.

"Yeah," said Jim brightly. "We could be backup."

Kim held her grappling hook high. "Okay. *Back up*," she demanded.

Shoulders slumping, the twins stepped back. Kim fired the hook. *Chunk!* The grappling hook struck high up the rock wall. Kim glanced at Ron and the boys.

"Don't touch *anything,*" said Kim. Then she allowed the line to reel her up. Straining, she began to climb the cliff, moving from one handhold to the next.

She never noticed the hidden camera built into the rock face. It hummed as it moved, tracking her progress, and sending her picture straight to the screen in Drakken's lair!

CHAPTER 7

Drakken's Dodo

Inside Drakken's lair, Kim Possible's image filled the large security screen. But Dr. Drakken didn't notice. The mad scientist was bent over a lab table, feverishly working on a new compliance chip.

Like a surgeon, he extended one hand to Shego. "Micrometer. . . ." he demanded.

"Yes, Dr. Drakken," said Shego and put the micrometer in his palm.

He worked a moment. Then his hand

came out again. "Nano-weld resistor."

"Yes, Dr. Drakken," said Shego. She gave him the tool, then waited for his next order.

With a gleam in his eye, Dr. Drakken smirked. "I love this," he said. "Hand me a fork."

"Yes, Dr. Drakken," said Shego. She searched the next room and returned with a fork.

Drakken waved the fork with glee. "Ha-ha! Get me a dodo bird," he ordered.

"Yes, Dr. Drakken," said Shego, as sweetly as ever.

With delight, Drakken watched his evil

sidekick frantically search the lab for a dodo bird.

He *still* had no clue that, on the screen behind him, Kim was climbing closer to his lair's entrance!

"Psych!" he finally cried at Shego. "Dodo birds are extinct. Oh, I'm being silly. . . ."

Drakken called Shego back and held up a new postage stamp-sized microchip. "There. I'm already done. A new compliance chip . . . isn't it lovely?" he asked.

Shego stared at the screen behind

Drakken. "Yes, it is lovely," she chanted.

Drakken scowled. "Can't you show a little more enthusiasm?" he complained.

"Hoo-rah," she said as her finger slowly pointed at the image of Kim Possible.

Drakken turned and recoiled in surprise.

"Kim Possible!" he hissed. She was climbing up the cliff. And she was almost at their front door! Drakken whirled on Shego. "Why didn't you tell me?" he demanded.

"I was looking for a dodo bird," she said.

His face fell. All right, he thought, *maybe* he deserved that one.

Hands behind his back, he furiously paced. He had to foil this uninvited crime-fighting guest. But *how*?

"Wait!" he cried as an idea dawned on him. "This is *delicious*."

As Kim pulled herself up to the final ledge, the rock wall in front of her swung away.

Drakken stood there. He smiled. *"Hello,"* he said.

Kim gasped. Before she could move, Drakken's gloved hand plunked his brand-new compliance chip onto her forehead.

* * *

Meanwhile, down on the jungle floor, everyone waited patiently for Kim.

Well, actually, it was *Ron* doing the patient waiting. The twins *never* did anything with patience.

"I'm bored," complained Tim.

Relaxing happily against a tree, Ron shared his philosophy: "Bored is good. Bored is safe."

"No, it's not," Jim said firmly as he hopped to his feet. "It's *boring.* Kim's taking forever."

Tim agreed. "We should go up there and see what's going on."

Ron sprang in front of the twins and cried, "Whassup, mama, Kim said to stay put!"

"Well, Kim's not here," Tim said.

"Yes, I am," called a familiar voice.

Ron, Rufus, and the twins spun to see Kim standing in front of them. Only, something wasn't quite right—Kim's eyes were glazed. And she wore a green-and-black jumpsuit.

"Kim, why are you dressed like Shego?" asked Ron uneasily.

"That is not important," Kim informed him.

Ron shrugged. "Okay. So where's the chip?" he asked.

Jim and Tim went wide-eyed. Together they cried, "On her forehead!"

The chip pulsed bright red. And slowly the mind-controlled Kim advanced with these *so* not happy words—

"Dr. Drakken will see you now."

CHAPTER 8

Ron to the Rescue

Ron handed Rufus to the twins and said, "Hold my naked mole rat, boys. I'm goin' in."

Vaulting forward, Ron landed in his most fearsome *BOO-YA!* battle pose.

"Gimme the chip," commanded Ron.

Swishing his arms to distract her with his righteous Ron-Fu, he darted close to Kim, then danced away. "Where's this hand goin'?" he teased. "Are you watching this hand? Then this one comes up and—"

Kim tossed him easily with a basic judo move. He crash-landed between the boys.

Rufus felt Ron's pain: "Ah-huh, *ow*!" cried the naked mole rat.

Jim glanced down at Ron. "Did you really think it would be that easy?" he asked.

"Well, I hoped," Ron said with a sigh.

Kim leaped and landed in front of her best friend. "Dr. Drakken has ordered the capture of Ron Stoppable," she declared.

"He remembered my name!" said Ron brightly.

The twins glanced at each other. Ron had tried and failed. Now it was their turn.

"Initiate big sister capture sequence!" commanded Tim.

"And we can't even get in trouble for it!" noted Jim.

"Sweet!" said Tim.

Jim and Tim tossed Rufus to Ron and broke into a run. Jim scaled a nearby tree, while Tim skidded past his startled sister.

"Get ready!" cried Tim. He snatched up the parachute's backpack and hurled it to his brother.

Jim caught it and jumped, closing the open parachute beneath Kim's feet like a snare net, trapping Kim.

Tim leaped and grabbed hold of his brother's dangling feet. Together they hauled

the trapped and struggling Kim into the air. "Gotcha!" they cried.

"You captured Kim Possible!" declared Ron. *Badical!*

Jim and Tim braced the backpack around the tree. "No big," they replied.

But inside the parachute trap, Kim had already ignited her laser pen. She burned through the fabric and clawed her way out with machine-like determination.

She was no longer Kim Possible. She was the Kim-inator and she would *not* stop—until she had her Stoppable!

The twins, Ron, and Rufus all raced up the tree branches!

Below them, Kim stomped through the jungle, looking for them.

"Must capture Ron Stoppable. Must capture Ron Stoppable. Must capture Ron Stoppable," Kim repeated.

Ron frowned. "If Kim were *not* under Drakken's control," he said, "she'd cook up a plan."

Rufus nodded enthusiastically. "A plan, uh-huh," he mumbled.

"Let yourself get captured," suggested Jim.

With a high startled *eeep*, Rufus fearfully zipped himself into Ron's pocket.

"A plan that doesn't involve *that*," said Ron.

"Drakken doesn't know about us," Tim explained. "He ordered Kim to get *you*, so that's all she cares about."

"Let her take you into his lair," said Jim. "We'll follow."

"Oh, and get the Kimmunicator," Tim told Ron.

Ron and Rufus brightened with hope. "To call for help!" Ron guessed.

With a nod, Rufus agreed: "Umm-ummm, good plan, um-um, yea."

Jim shook his head. "No," he said. "We can take the power cell out of the Kimmunicator—"

Tim held out their homemade masterpiece and added, "And put it in—"

"Our silicon phase disruptor—" said Jim.

"Which will jam the control frequency of that chip," his brother finished. He reached over and slipped a rope from Ron's utility belt.

Jim smiled and noted, "That's why Bortle had a disruptor in his lab—"

"To override the chip!" concluded Tim as he tied the rope around a thick branch.

Ron shuddered and told them, "This finishing each other's sentences thing is really freaking me out."

"Here she comes!" said Tim.

"Go!" said Jim.

Ron squealed as he plunged through the air. He hung down in front of Kim, dangling from the homemade bungee cord.

"What up, Kim?" asked Ron nervously. "So how's the whole mind control thing workin' out?"

She unhooked him and hauled him down. "You must be taken to Dr. Drakken," she announced.

Welcome to humiliation nation, thought Ron as Kim dragged him away.

In Drakken's lair, the scientist paced.

"You are very smart, and look good in this light," Shego told her crazed boss.

“Fine, Shego, don’t wear it out,” Drakken muttered.

Just then, Kim appeared at the cave’s entrance. “Dr. Drakken,” she said, “you are very smart, and look good in this light.”

Drakken turned to Shego. “Now see,” he said, pointing to Kim, “*she* sells it.”

Beside Kim, Ron stood with his hands tied behind his back. Peeking out of Ron’s pocket, Rufus located the Kimmunicator on a table. Excited, he dropped down to grab it.

Drakken didn't notice. He was too excited about Kim's following his beastly order.

"So, Kim Possible," said Drakken, "you climbed down the waterfall and captured your very best friend. I like this mind control thing very much."

"Yes, Dr. Drakken," Kim said sweetly.

Drakken was tickled pink—which was really something for a guy whose skin was *blue*.

"Good," he said. "Now go secure the perimeter or something."

Kim pointed. "What about the hairless rodent?" she asked.

Dr. Drakken finally saw Rufus dragging the Kimmunicator across a workbench.

"Stop!" bellowed Drakken. He held out his hand. "Give me that."

Unhappily, Rufus turned over the Kimmunicator.

"Good," Drakken said. "Now, Shego, Kim . . . destroy that little bald thing."

Kim and Shego marched ominously toward Rufus.

Rufus quivered. "*Wa-oh!*" he cried.

CHAPTER 9

Tweebs Triumphant!

Shego came at Rufus from the left. And Kim came at him from the right. But the clever mole rat leaped into the air and the girls smashed together!

Coming down, Rufus bounced off Kim's head, then Shego's, and finally darted away.

Meanwhile, Drakken had *no idea* that Jim and Tim had already entered his lair. Not until Jim sprung into view.

"Who are *you*?" demanded Drakken.

"A kid who's gonna *bring you down*," Jim declared.

"Oh, really? You and what army?" Drakken said with a smirk.

"Whoo-sha!" roared Tim as he rocketed out of the darkness and bounded onto the scientist's back.

Drakken glimpsed the twin's face during the struggle and gasped. "A clone!"

Tim clamped his hands over the evil genius's eyes. "Yeah, that's right, loser."

As Drakken flailed, Jim seized the

Kimmunicator from his belt and ran. Tim quickly followed.

"Shego, Kim! Forget about the rodent!" commanded Drakken. "Get those little clones!"

A dozen feet away, Jim told Ron, "Stall 'em."

"Right. Okay," Ron said. His hands still bound behind his back, Ron blocked Shego and Kim.

Shego's green glowing energy claws swept at Ron.

Ron sprang into the air and yanked his hands in front of him as he touched down. When Shego struck next, her claws carved the ropes and freed him!

Ron sprinted from the girls into a long cave with two doors at the end. He escaped

through the door on the left. But Shego and the Kim-inator were in hot pursuit.

Ron hid among the huge orb-shaped machines in Drakken's lab. He nibbled nervously on his gloved fingers as Kim and Shego stalked him.

Rufus chittered and pointed at a slab with a small podium. The word ELEVATOR was etched in the wall behind it. *Good goin', little dude!* thought Ron.

While the girls peered within the orbs' hatches, Ron and Rufus snuck to the platform. Ron tapped at buttons until the platform shot up with a *whoosh*!

As Ron and Rufus zoomed to the lair's top floor, Shego and Kim leaped into action. In an amazing display of acrobatics, the two leapfrogged up to the moving platform.

Quickly, Ron flew off the platform and onto a catwalk.

"Don't look down," Ron reminded himself. "Don't look down. Don't look dowwwwaahhhhh!"

He looked down—and fell through a grate into a long dark tunnel. With a not-so-manly shriek, he slid through the steel slide.

Meanwhile, in the lab, the twins raced around and around Dr. Drakken. The dizzied

Drakken clutched his aching noodle. He couldn't *take* this!

Suddenly, Ron and Rufus dropped from an air duct in the ceiling. They landed at Drakken's feet.

Yikes! Leaping up, the two scrambled backward, right into a metal door.

Whoosh! The door rose. Shego and Kim circled Ron and Rufus, ready to attack.

"Everybody stop!" the twins cried.

Dr. Drakken spun to face the twins. "I'm on to you," he told them. "You're not clones. You're just garden-variety twins. *You* don't give the orders here."

"I do if I've got a silicon phase disruptor," Jim said confidently.

"A silicon phase disruptor?" repeated Drakken worriedly. *"Really?"*

"Whoo-sha," said Tim.

Drakken stopped. "Wait," he said. "How could two little boys carry a silicon phase disrupter up the cliff?"

Jim and Tim proudly brandished their handheld unit. "It's portable!" declared Tim.

Drakken sneered and said, "*Portable?* Oh, you really had me going there for a moment."

The twins smiled knowingly. Tim pointed the disruptor at Kim and Shego.

He tapped the red button on the phase disruptor. But nothing happened!

"Oh," said Jim with alarm.

Tim jabbed the button again and again. Still nothing! "Uh-oh," he said softly.

Drakken howled in triumph. "Ah! Ah! Ha-ha-ha! Portable silicon phase disrupter. I *knew* it couldn't be done!"

Ron yelled to the twins, "Are you *sure* the batteries are in right? The plus goes with the plus thing and little slash goes with the other *not* plus."

Jim and Tim exchanged glances, then quickly reversed the batteries. Tim raised the device again.

This time when Tim hit the red button, a stream of blue-white energy burst forward,

striking the chips on Kim and Shego's foreheads. The chips sparked, then popped off their victims and fell to the floor.

Kim blinked as she came to her senses. Beside her, Shego also snapped to attention. She surveyed Kim's new clothes.

"Nice outfit," Shego noted sarcastically.

Kim smirked. "Nice apron."

Shego peered down. Furious, she tore off her silly frilly apron and stormed toward Drakken.

"Okay, Doc," she snarled, "for future reference, the chip made me obey *every* command. But I was *aware* of exactly what was happening."

Dr. Drakken winced. "The whole time?"

Shego drew closer, her teeth clenched. "Dodge ball and *dodos*!?"

The evil doctor nervously backed away. "Ooooo," he whimpered.

"Do you have *any* idea what listening to you is like?" she shouted. "It is so *boring*."

Drakken bolted, but Shego was hot on his heels. Then the pair rounded a corner and vanished.

"Shouldn't we go after them?" asked Ron.

Kim giggled and said, "Nah, whatever Shego's going to do to Drakken is ten times worse than anything I could come up with."

"I'm sure Jim and Tim could think of something cruel and unusual," noted Ron.

Kim gave her brothers a serious look and said, "I think Jim and Tim have come up with enough ideas for one day." Then she broke into a wide smile. "And every one of them

rocked! For tweebs, you guys are pretty amazing."

Even Rufus was touched. "*Awww . . .*" he said.

Kneeling, Kim gave both of her brothers a big hug.

"Ew, *gross*," said the boys, squirming.

"Are you feeling okay?" Jim asked Kim.

Snatching up the compliance chips, Kim got to her feet. "C'mon," she said, still smiling. "Let's get out of here."

CHAPTER 10

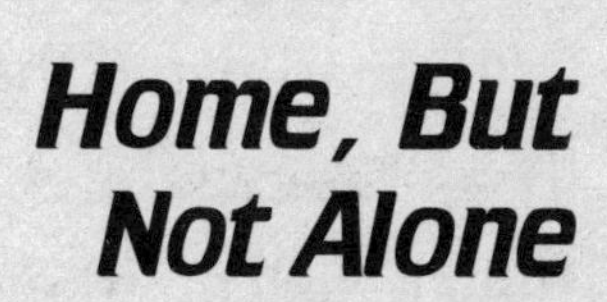

Home, But Not Alone

It was late when Kim heard her parents' car pull into the driveway.

"Hey, everybody! Good news!" declared Kim's dad as he strode into the family room. "Our marriage is stronger than ever, and we caught a mess of trout."

Kim's mom took in the sight of the twins sleeping on the couch beside Kim. Smiling, she said, "It looks like somebody took very good care of her little brothers."

Kim adjusted the blanket covering Jim and Tim. "Awww . . ." she whispered. "When they're asleep like this, they hardly seem evil at all."

"You were ten once, too, Kimmie," Kim's mother reminded her.

Kim shrugged and said, "Yeah, but I wasn't as bad as *them.*"

Her parents exchanged serious looks.

Kim tensed. "Was I?" she asked.

"You were . . . *spirited,*" her mother told her.

"No babysitter alive could handle you," Kim's Dad blurted out. "Not that we could find anyone *willing* to try after a certain point."

Kim's mom knelt next to the couch. She brushed the bangs away from Jim's eyes. Then she frowned. "Honey?" she asked. "What have the boys got on their foreheads?"

Whoops! Kim quickly aimed the phase disruptor at her brothers' foreheads and hit the red button.

FZZZZ-ZZZZZ!

Just like that, the two mind-control chips Kim had taken from Drakken popped off the twins' heads.

Instantly, their eyes sprang open. The two leaped off the couch and chased each other,

throwing pillows, cushions, and pretty much anything within reach.

"Can't catch me!" hollered Jim.

Tim smacked him with one of the heavier cushions. "Oh, yes I can!" he yelled.

Kim leaned back and checked out her parents. Their eyes widened as the twins tore up the place.

"I finally understand how special my brothers are," Kim admitted seriously. "And I love them to bits. But sometimes . . ." Her eyebrow arched. "*Nothing* says 'bedtime' like a little mind control."

Kim had a feeling that her parents just might come around to agreeing with her.

After all, anything was possible . . . for a Possible.